PERMANENT VERN

- A SHORT STORY -

WRITTEN & ILLUSTRATED BY
TIM DEMOSS

Telling a story is like reaching into a granary full of wheat and drawing out a handful. There is always more to tell than can be told... there is also more than needs to be told, and more than anybody wants to hear.

- WENDELL BERRY, *JAYBER CROW*

CONTENTS

CHAPTER 1: VERN

Vern was four inches tall and lived in a small felted area beneath the notes A3 and B4 of the Baldwin piano in the unused upstairs guest room in the home of Vasili and Melpo Melopolous in rural Pennsylvania. The room was small. Other than Vern's piano, the only piece of furniture was a hard-backed mustard yellow reading-chair, which sat in the corner against built-in bookshelves. Vern, though fond of reading, had no use for such an enormous chair. When the urge to read struck him (which happened less and less these days; he was very busy), he would remove one of the lighter volumes from the Bottom Shelf, lay it open on the pool-green carpet, and carefully lie down on the pages. It was delicate work.

Downstairs, the coffee maker hissed and

burbled. Melpo's morning routine was religious; at six the hiss-and-burble of her coffee maker traveled through the kitchen, up through the lathe and plaster of the walls, and into Vern's room, where the sounds and smells would wake him up, regular as clockwork. This was convenient for Vern, as the actual clock in the upstairs room had ceased to function in any non-decorative capacity long before he had come to live there. No one had come to fix it. In fact, no one but Vern had seen the clock, or the room, in over eight years.

Vern scratched his eyes and sat up, leaning against the dark red felt that lined his home. His room within the piano was sparsely decorated. A clean, white sock with red on the toe made for his bed. An old quarter on a die served as his nightstand. Across the room a Post-It with some writing was tacked to the wall. Vern walked sleepily over to read it. Here is what it said.

TO DO:
   – READ LIST
   – GO DOWN
   – WRITE
   – COME BACK
   – SLEEP

The first object done, Vern stretched, exited the piano, and began the second.

He made his way to a small hole in the wall behind the piano. This hole was the only imperfection in the room. Vern had created it himself, as he had been able to think of no other feasible way to access the lower floor of the house. He had tried his best to make the hole as neat as possible.

Vern leaned into the hole and felt around until his hands touched a thin pipe. He shimmied downwards until a glow and the smell of Melpo's coffee began to appear beneath him. He approached the glow and, walking through it, entered his recording studio.

His studio was on top of Vasili and Melpo's

refrigerator. It consisted of a small chair (a zip-lock bag filled with beans), a pad of yellow Post-Its, and a nub of a pencil. Vern shook his head to clear it, arranged himself comfortably on his bean-chair, and wrote the date neatly on the top of the Post-It. Satisfied, he began to observe. It was six-fifteen precisely.

Melpo, as usual, helped Vasili walk from their bedroom to his chair facing the television. Vasili was an old man and had been ill as long as Vern had been living there. He was usually confined to his chair. Melpo was even older than Vasili, and probably just as sick, but out of stubbornness she lived her life as if she were not. Thus it was that after bringing Vasili to his chair, she returned to the kitchen to pour him a cup of coffee. Vern scratched a note down. His Post-It now read:

> – 14 April, 8
> – 6:15AM. Business as usual. Black mug w/ gold handle for V. Floral for M.

The television came to life. A pretty young meteorologist began explaining the weather. Vern's pencil flew.

> *– The weather girl is new. Will have to see if old one is sick or being replaced.*

He looked up as Melpo gently placed Vasili's coffee down, then sat down on the chair beside him.

"Thank you, Mel," he muttered, as he closed his eyes. Melpo smiled. On the screen, the meteorologist announced that her name was Noelle Montgomery, filling in for Madison James. Madison was out sick.

> *– Name: Noelle Montgomery. Madison James (regular) is out sick. Will note tomorrow.*

Melpo and Vasili watched their morning news in comfortable silence. Vern took this opportunity to examine the room. Had anything changed? It didn't appear as if anything had. Nothing needed to. The owners were, like Vern, quite set in their ways. A year ago they had replaced their carpet. Three years ago they had been given a new coffee maker. (On her first morning with the new machine, Melpo couldn't figure out how to get it to work, and consequently Vern had overslept by an hour and a quarter.) Those were the only two Big Changes that Vern could remember. Most days had No Changes, or maybe a Small Change - a new mug, a re-arrangement of furniture, or a change in the evening's entertainment. But on the whole, Melpo and Vasili lived in the comfortable state of people who had found what suited them and no longer needed the drug of variety. Vern leaned back in his chair and smiled. He could not have been more at home.

By noon his Post-It looked like this:

> *– 14 April, 8*
> *– 6:15AM. Business as usual. Black mug w/ gold handle for V. Floral for M.*

– *The weather girl is new. Will have to see if old one is sick or being replaced.*

– *Name: Noelle Montgomery. Madison James (regular) is out sick. Will note tomorrow.*

– *Raining. Began at 7:30AM. Pitter-patter.*

– *8AM. Breakfast. Toast. Jam = Dunlop's Blackberry. Conversation centered around granddaughter Leila. Birthday is Friday. M wants V to sign the card.*

– *9AM. M took a walk around the house and came back with flowers. Vase placed on table between her and V's chairs.*

– *10AM. M helped V walk to the bathroom. M swept the kitchen and began to sew.*

– *11AM. M sewing. V sleeping. M turned off TV.*

– *Noon. M still sewing. Made a mis-stitch and had to undo about twenty minutes of work.*

He stretched and yawned. If he had been the sort of creature to eat or drink, he would have enjoyed a cup of coffee. Recording was often tiresome work. Predictable, too - he could usually guess nine out of ten things that Melpo and Vasili would do.

"But," Vern thought to himself, "one never knows what the tenth thing will be." And so he sat there. He was happy to.

It was a good thing that the aging couple had only three rooms in the main portion of their home; he wasn't sure how he could possibly keep track of their activity had there been any more of them.

His notes continued.

> – 1PM. M and V worked on the flower puzzle. About forty percent done. The piece that fell on the floor yesterday is still there.
> – 2PM. Puzzle.
> – 3PM. Naps.
> – 4PM. Still napping. A package

came.

– 5PM. M began dinner. Mashed potatoes, rotisserie chicken, French beans. Cherry juice. Typical place settings. Tall glasses. No ice today.

– 6PM. Dinner. Phone call from daughter Eleanor. V was tired and went to watch TV while M chatted. Conversation lasted twenty minutes. E updated M on their recent move to Florida.

– 7PM. M and V watched Jeopardy. As usual, V knew a surprising amount of the answers. M adores him.

– 8PM. M walked V to bed. M came out and sewed.

– 9PM. M went to bed.

Vern scrunched his eyes and yawned again. An uneventful day. Yesterday he had recorded a dropped puzzle piece, a broken plate, and a power outage. Maybe he was due for a slow streak.

He peeled the Post-It off of the pad and ascended the pipe into his room. He tugged a thick book from the Bottom Shelf and laid it carefully on the carpet. (Before being appropriated, this book had once been an English language usage dictionary.) With great effort, he opened it to the middle. He stepped up onto the pages, and - between *hoard* and *hoi polloi* - firmly placed the Post-It. It sat in a row with two others, dated 12 April and 11 April. Above this row sat April 10, 9, and 8. And so forth.

Each note carried, in Vern's delicate, precise hand, an account of the day's proceedings at the Melopolous house. Some days were marked with a bold underline for a Small Change. The last Big Change - Melpo's new coffee maker - had occurred between *billion* and *bimonthly*. Most days, like today, were left unmarked. No Noticeable Changes. Satisfied, Vern closed the book and repositioned it in its place on the Bottom Shelf.

He mentally checked his to-do list. In his mind, it looked like this:

TO DO:
- ~~*READ LIST*~~
- ~~*GO DOWN*~~
- ~~*WRITE*~~
- ~~*COME BACK*~~
- *SLEEP*

It was closing time. He scanned the room. The books were still lined up; the chair was there; it was still raining outside. Everything was fine. Vern scurried up the leg of his piano, tucked himself into the red-toed sock, and shut his eyes.

Chapter 2: A Change

It was bright inside the piano. This was the first thing Vern noticed when his eyes re-opened, but it took him a moment to realize why. The piano lid was open.

Vern snapped out of bed and stood, staring, at the popcorn ceiling. Who had opened the lid? It must have been Melpo. Had she not made coffee? Why was she upstairs? And furthermore, the light - even with the lid open, it shouldn't be this bright - a quick glance out the window sent Vern into an even greater state of alarm - it was nearly ten o'clock. Three hours late! This would never do. Three hours, lost forever. Who knew what had happened when he was off his watch?

He dropped down the piano leg and rushed

for his hole in the wall. He had nearly reached it when he paused; then slowly, he walked back out into the main portion of the room. He looked up at the bookshelf. Two, three, maybe four holes dotted the shelves. Books removed! Which ones had they been? He had meant to make a catalog, months ago, and he felt his heart sink into the carpet. He did not know which books had been lost.

They must have been taken downstairs - but they hadn't had any visitors yesterday, and M and V didn't like stairs - someone must have arrived this morning - he turned away from the bookshelf, and saw something new. It was silhouetted by the window, and it was holding a small pile of books. It knelt down on the ground.

"Hello," it said. "My name is Mallory."

Chapter 3: Mallory

Mallory's eyes were blue and rimmed with thin wire glasses. She was old and gray and had a small scar under her left eye; Vern thought he might have recognized her from some get-together at the house a few years prior. A friend of M and V. As she knelt down, she cast a shadow over the shag carpet and the still-standing Vern. Her glasses refracted the sunlight into two rainbow pools that danced around his feet.

"Hello," she repeated. "What's your name?"

Vern told her.

"How long have you lived here?"

He wasn't sure. It had been at least eight years. That was when he'd begun to keep track, anyway.

"Keep track of what?"

Vern began to grow impatient.
"Every morning, I sit in my studio -"

"Your studio?"

"-I sit in my studio, downstairs, and I write down what Melpo and Vasili do. How they're feeling. What they eat, and so on."

Mallory shuffled her weight and began to squat on her heels. She placed the stack of books to one side.

"Why?" she asked.

Vern was trying to read the titles on the spines of the books, in case she suddenly left with them, and so he didn't hear her question. She had to repeat it.

"Why?"

"Why what?"

"Why do you write all this?"

"Why does anyone write?" he answered. "So we can remember what happened."

Vern scampered to the bookshelf and dragged the dictionary onto the floor.

"Here, you see?" he called, as he opened the book to a random page. "October eleventh of last year. 9AM, Melpo spilled a pot of cold coffee on the living room carpet" - here he looked up and addressed Mallory directly - "the red plush one they used to have. It was replaced the same week with the one they've got now."

Mallory stared at him. He was a curious creature. Aside from the obvious abnormality of his size, he had eyes and ears that were much too large for his face, hair that swish-swashed in front of his eyes, and a mouse-like tail. He wore a tattered burgundy vest (which fit perfectly) over a navy blue sweater (which was far too large and extended past his knees). His feet, which resembled paws more than anything human, were bare.

His large eyes stared back at her. "Go on.
Give me another date."

"July 18th, last year."

Had Mallory requested July 17th or 19th,
she would have heard of The Great Refrigerator Defrosting or The Porch Package
Thief, respectively. The 18th, however, had
no such story. In fact, to Vern's shame, his
records that day were sparse. They began at
11AM instead of his usual six-fifteen. Melpo
had been sick and as such the coffee had not
been made. Consequently, Vern had slept in.
Vasili had watched television, or sat sleeping
and facing the television, for the entire day,
except to get Melpo her meals or bring her
some cold water.

Mallory, who by now was sitting cross-
legged on the carpet, reached out and
turned the dictionary, with Vern on top of
it, to face her. She examined the Post-Its -
thankfully, thought Vern, with reverence.
Admiration, even.

Her examination went on for some time. Then -

"You do this every day?"

"I do."

"Since when?"

Vern chewed the inside of his cheek, then shrugged.

Mallory lifted the left page.

"May I?"

Vern slid off the book and down to the floor.

Mallory turned the pages, one by one at first, then in clumps, passing *flagrant* and *flack*, *cripple* and *crescendo*, reaching the As of *alibi*, *albeit*, and finally *a/an*, and continuing into the Preface, where the Post-Its abruptly stopped. Mallory began to read out loud. The entry was short.

– 21 March, 1.

– Melpo and Vasili had company today - their daughter Eleanor and her new husband Matt came by for lunch.

– No other changes.

"It's a short entry," Vern explained. "It was the first one. Hadn't found my groove yet."

"What did you do on the 20th? The day before?" she asked.

He hung his head. "I don't know. I didn't write it down."

Mallory squinted. "Something must have happened to make you want to start this?" She tapped a finger on the book.

"I didn't write it down," Vern repeated. "It's conjecture."

"What is?"

"There's no record of it. I have thoughts

19

about why I started. But it's only hindsight. I can't say for sure."

He scrambled back onto the book and pointed. "So I keep writing so in the future I'll know what happened."

Mallory silently read a few more of the early Post-Its. Suddenly she turned to Vern.

"These are all about Melpo and Vasili?"

"Yes. And others who come here."

She put her hands on her knees and sat up.

"Do you write about you?"

Vern blinked. "About me?"

"Yes. You write what Melpo and Vasili do. Do you write down what you do?"

Vern thought about this before answering. "I suppose writing down what M and V do is what I do. If I ever miss a morning - like I

am right now - I write that down too. See -"
he pointed to a Post-It note halfway down
the Preface.

He read it out loud:

> – *April 1, 1.*
> – *I overslept by an hour.*
> – *8AM. Melpo went to the garden.*

Vern stopped reading as he began to grow
anxious. He had reminded himself yet
again of his missing duty downstairs. And
he would need a record of his conversation
with Mallory too. He glanced at her watch.
Ten-thirty. He sighed. Mallory noticed.

"Are you late?"

"Yes. More than three hours."

"You always start at six-fifteen?"

"I aim to. If you'll excuse me-"

"Why don't you start earlier?"

Vern looked up. "Excuse me?"

Mallory continued. "What if something happens at five forty-five? How will you record it then?"

"I start at six-fifteen because that's when their routine starts," Vern explained with a whisper of wounded professional pride. "I'm finite; I have to sleep, I can't record everything."

"No," said Mallory, softly. "You can't."

Vern became indignant. "See here -"

Mallory ignored him. "Do you ever go outside?"

Vern shuddered. "I tried, the first year."

"You tried? What was wrong with it?"

"There's too much to keep track of. Birds. Melpo's garden and the little pond. The weather. The neighbors." He pointed to these words which were scattered on the Post-Its around him. "I could never keep it all straight. I gave it up."

Almost as if summoned by Vern's description, a pair of cardinals began to call through the window. Mallory became distracted. She walked to the window and turned the little hand-crank. A breath of fresh air came in, as did the cardinals' song. Mallory breathed. Once, twice.

She turned to Vern and smiled. He was standing a few feet closer to her than he had before. The dictionary lay behind him. The light sound of shuffling paper could be heard as the breeze gently lifted and set down a dozen Post-Its. She walked to him and slowly extended her hand. He stepped into it. Her palms were dry and cracked; she carried him in the one and used the other to open the door to the Downstairs.

Chapter 4: The Garden

The garden was nothing like Vern remembered. The pond had been filled in and a bed of lavender had taken its place. There was a butterfly bush and a stone birdbath. There was a path of stone pavers with imprints of little baby feet and initials of little baby names. The path led to a gazebo - a *gazebo* - complete with a small table and pair of chairs. In these chairs sat Melpo and Vasili, laughing and playing cards. Mallory walked in their direction.

"Isn't it lovely?" she asked.

"When did that gazebo get here?" he asked, weakly.

"I'm sure I don't know. It's new to me since the last time I was here."

Vern's head swam. He had been foolish to leave the outdoors uncataloged. He had convinced himself to leave it alone, that it would be better that way than to attempt the impossible. He looked around the brim of Mallory's hand, took in the sights, and became more and more sure that he had made a mistake in abandoning them.

As they neared the gazebo, Vern's despair melted into a quiet confidence. He had made a mistake, yes - but what new avenues of work this opened up! His days had been slow lately. He was a talented enough recorder to begin tracking indoor and outdoors both. Mallory was right - why *did* he start at six-fifteen? He could wake up earlier, stay up later, write more - he could use two Post-Its, one for inside, one for outside. He could even try to back-catalog the things he had missed.

Visions of more and more Post-Its filling more and more books flew before Vern's eyes. Today was no longer a defeat. It was the beginning of a golden era, one of ever-more robust and methodical recording. Vern smiled at the thought of it.

"Mal!" called Vasili, from the gazebo. "Come join!"

She waved the hand that wasn't holding Vern. "What does it look like I'm doing?"

She paused, knelt to the ground, and extended her hand to the grass.

"I assume," she said in a low voice, "that you'd like to remain a secret."

"Historically that's how it's been," said Vern, gratefully, as he dismounted.

She offered her pinky for him to shake. "So long. Can you find your way back upstairs?"

He nodded. "I'm short on practice, but I'll get used to it. There's a drainpipe, or there used to be."

He watched her walk away, her blue dress swishing around her ankles. He listened as she joined Melpo and Vasili; from the rock he sat on, he could see the three of them quite well. He became engrossed in their conversation. He heard about Mallory's family and about the health of their mutual friends; he heard, finally, the details of that bothersome neighbor with the drum set; he learned that Mallory's sister was the one who had invented the pickle recipe Melpo used each summer; and of course he heard all of the useless but interesting things that come up when three old friends talk about nothing at all. It was only after an hour or so of this that Vern realized that he'd forgotten both his pencil and his stack of Post-Its.

A brief moment of worry filled his heart. It was replaced almost immediately with the smell of the moss on the rock where he sat, then again soon after by the desire to take a walk. He listened to the conversation for a few moments more; then, as the desire became less and less resistible, he hopped off the rock and began to walk through the garden.

He padded along and closed his eyes. As he walked, he heard over his shoulder the voices of Melpo, Vasili, and Mallory, distinct at first, then blending together into a single murmur, almost indistinguishable from the rest of the buzzes and breezes that filled the outdoors. As he listened to this new song, Vern thought to himself he had never heard anything so fine as the sounds of the world unmarred by the scraping of a pencil.

THE END